Lilien Wise

My Three Jewels and Other Poems

Lilien Wise

My Three Jewels and Other Poems

ISBN/EAN: 9783743388598

Manufactured in Europe, USA, Canada, Australia, Japa

Cover: Foto ©Andreas Hilbeck / pixelio.de

Manufactured and distributed by brebook publishing software
(www.brebook.com)

Lilien Wise

My Three Jewels and Other Poems

" How fair the simple flowers appear,
    If hands belov'd the garland braid,
 And friendship's flowers collected here—
    Tho' Springs must die—*will never fade!*"

MY THREE JEWELS

AND

OTHER POEMS.

LILIEN WISE.

SAN FRANCISCO:
H. S. CROCKER & COMPANY,
Printers and Stationers,
1887.

Contents.

—

Selections.

CONTENTS.

My Three Jewels.

Three Jewels of immortal birth,
Three Jewels bright, of priceless worth,
Three Jewels I can call my own,
As bright as ever decked a crown.
Each Jewel in a casket lies,
And each and all I highly prize.

The first, a "Diamond," sparkling bright,
Of the first water in my sight;
And though six years I've called it mine,
I scarce begin to note the time,
It seems so short, since first I pressed
The darling treasure to my breast;
And ever since, with tender care,
I've fondly smiled to see it there.

The second is a lovely "Pearl,"
So sweet you'd think it was a girl;
The world could not produce another,
And yet it is the Diamond's brother.
Oh, such a Jewel! All that see
Think 'tis the finest of the three.

5

Then who can chide a mother's love,
If she a little partial prove?
And though all three dwell in my heart,
The " Pearl" can claim the largest part.

The third, a " Ruby " and a brother,
The very image of its mother,
And all who see it think me cruel,
Because 'tis not my fav'rite Jewel;
For ev'ry feature of the elf
Reflects the image of myself:
Its eyes, its mouth, and nose, and chin,
And e'en the color of its skin;
Its ways and manners, all so mild,
Proclaim the mother in the child;
But for my " Pearl " I feel more care,
Because I see its father there.

Whatever ills of life betide,
These Jewels rare shall be my pride;
To guard them and to keep them bright,
Each day shall be my chief delight,
And ev'ry prayer I send to Heav'n
Shall for their welfare here be giv'n,
That when time's furrows mark my brow,
They then may shine more bright than now,
And in my last declining day,
My *Jewels* light me on my way,
And 'round me shed their hallowed light,
'Till I shall bid the world "Good night."
*   *   *   *   *   *

Three Jewels bright to me were giv'n,
Three Jewels of immortal birth,
But one has been recalled to Heav'n,
And two are left with me on earth:
Three links united by my love,
Two angels here and one above.

Among the shining hosts above
A happy cherub there I see,
My darling boy, with sacred love
And beaming eye, smiles down on me;
Submissively I kiss the rod,
And give my darling back to God.

Though of my dearest hope bereft,
My heart in saddest mourning lies,
I'll try to live for those still left,
And fit them also for the skies;
That when our days on earth are o'er,
We'll meet in heav'n to part no more.

Gems.

A Polish superstition holds,
A certain gem our fate controls;
Each month a gem throughout the year
Unfolds to us our life's career.
Through custom on each natal day
Lovers nice compliment do pay,
Accompanied with present fine
In which the natal gem doth shine.

January.

GARNET. CONSTANCY.

This stone denotes a constant mind,
To truth, fidelity inclined.
All born this month may fitly claim
This splendid fortune and the name.

February.

AMETHYST. PEACE.

No furious passions fill the breast,
But peace gives ever constant rest.
If in this month your birthday be,
No sorrow will you ever see.

March.

BLOOD STONE.   COURAGE.

If born in March your courage bold
Through dangers great will life uphold,
And ev'ry enterprise in life
Shall bring success amidst the strife.

April.

DIAMOND.   INNOCENCE.

Innocent of guilt or harm,
This stone shall prove a constant charm,
The brightest gem that ever shone,
Innocence and this precious stone.

May.

EMERALD.   LOVE.

In May the emerald doth possess
The gift of love, complete success.
Of all the powers be this one thine,
For love sincere makes man divine.

June.

AGATE.   LONGEVITY.

The agate tells long life and health,
Two things, 'tis said, worth more than wealth;
For with the body full of pains
What good is all the rich man's gains.

9

July.

RUBY.   FORGETFULNESS.

Though friends prove untrue and lovers have fled,
Learn to live and forget, for it is truly said
That the ruby insures you a cure for all sorrow,
If you are jilted to-day you'll forget it to-morrow.

August.

SARDONYX.   HAPPINESS.

Thou shalt live in felicity, joy and content,
And ne'er know the sorrows of those who repent.
This stone will insure you felicity great
With the one you shall claim in life for a mate.

September.

CHRYSOLITE.   PROTECTION.

This stone will protect from the follies of youth,
And insure an old age supported by truth;
How blest to look back o'er your life and remember
You've peacefully lived, by your birth in September.

October.

OPAL.　　MISFORTUNE.

Though misfortune o'ertake you and shroud you in
　　gloom,
Hope brightens the future and smiles on the tomb;
Though life be all darkness and fortune may frown,
Hope points to the future and offers a crown.

November.

TOPAZ.　　FRIENDSHIP.

The topaz gives fidelity and friendship to mankind,
I'm sure no better jewel in the casket you can find,
And when the sere November of your life has come
　　at last
These will seem the sweetest virtues of the manhood
　　that is past.

December.

TURQUOIS.　　SUCCESS.

Success shall attend the turquois stone
If worn by the peasant or king on the throne!
Then cherish this jewel as one of the best;
On the finger of diligence ever 'tis blest!

All Right.

I have a little cherub boy,
   His eyes are dark as night,
And 'tis his mother's greatest joy
   To hear him say, "All right."

But nine short months have swiftly flown,
   Since first he saw the light,
And yet in baby prattling tone
   He sweetly says, "All right."

The dearest wish my fond heart knows,
   Of blessings rich and bright,
Shall be that as he older grows,
   He still shall say, "All right."

And when at last Time's sure decay
   Shall dim my failing sight,
I'll think of him, as now,
   And say, "I know he is all right."

Floral Fortune-Teller.

January.

OAK GERANIUM.   FRIENDSHIP.

How sweet it is to know we have a friend
On whom in weal or woe we may depend,
For friendship, like a soothing balm, contains
A never failing cure for all our pains.

February.

HAWTHORN.   HOPE.

Hope, like an anchor, doth sustain,
When tossed on life's tempestuous main;
It gives the cloud a silver lining,
And keeps the heart from sad repining.

March.

HYACINTH.   FAITH.

Faith is the evidence of things not seen,
It makes the Christain's life on earth serene.
Faith scorns to hold one doubt or jealous fear,
But full of trust, confides in friends so dear.

13

April.

MYRRH.   GLADNESS.

How brightly arises the day star of gladness,
Dispelling the gloom that surrounds us in sadness,
And filling the heart with its rays of delight,
As the sun brings the day and dispels the dark night.

May.

STAR OF BETHLEHEM.   PURITY.

Angels are robed in white, and purity dwells in heaven!
Mistaken souls; no boon like this to mortals here is
   given;
The best of earth are spotted with the stain of daily sin,
And naught but death can ever make erring mortal
   clean.

June.

DAILY ROSE.   SMILE.

How sweetly blooms the daily rose and sheds its fra-
   grance 'round,
So smiles of joy should wreath the lips wherever we
   are found.
A smile may gladden some poor soul and ease their
   bosom's pain,
And 't will not cost you but a thought but bring you
   joy again.

July.

BITTER SWEET.   TRUTH.

Truth is the mirror of the mind, revealing all within,
It shows defects of every kind e'en to the smallest sin.
"Truth crushed to earth will rise again" and conquer
      in the end;
Then make the truth thy constant guide, thy ever
      faithful friend.

August.

DAFFODIL.   CONTENTMENT.

Contentment of mind's a continual feast,
The great may possess it and so may the least
It belongs to the young just as well as the old,
But it cannot be purchased with silver or gold.

September.

BLUE BELL.   SOLITUDE.

The wise, the learned and the good seek solitude to
      think,
And there, in meditation deep, of solid comfort drink,
And from seclusion's secret vale bring forth some
      precious flower,
And plant it in life's sunny dale, to bloom for many
      an hour.

October.

CHINA ROSE.　GRACE.

Elegant manners and beautiful form,
Like the rose among flowers, have ever a charm;
Attracting the eye—and cause admiration,
For beauty is ever the queen of creation.

November.

LAUREL.　FAME.

The height of man's ambition is for fame
To win the laurels of a glorious name.
Though death should stand before his dauntless eyes,
He'll face the monster to obtain the prize.

December.

AMARANTH.　IMMORTALITY.

Immortal man, thy soul can never die,
Although thy body in the dust must lie.
Immortal life; the boundless thought is great,
That man should rise from dust to God's estate.

Alphabetical Acrostic.

Abstain from alcoholic drinks of every name and kind;
Beware of habits that debase the body and the mind.
Conform to nothing that you think wicked or impolite;
Do unto others what you know to be both kind and right.
Engage in nothing sinful, e'en to please your dearest friend;
Folly will bring its own reward, and punish in the end.
Give freely to the poor, for thus you're lending to the Lord;
Here He has promised in return, a pure and great reward,
In ev'rything you think and do, let honor be your guide;
Justice and truth and charity be evermore your pride.
Kind reader, if these simple rules you will adopt through life;
Let me predict, you'll thus avoid all ills and bitter strife.
Morning will dawn upon you then with pleasure on its wings;

17

Night, too, will bring, to cheer you on, so many happy
 things.

Or if a cloud of sorrow should envelop your bright
 way;

Press onward, for to-morrow may be a still brighter
 day.

Queens, too, and Kings their troubles have, and so
 have you and I;

Remember, 'tis the lot of man, for all were born to
 die.

Some die while they are in their youth. Perhaps a
 happy fate!

To others, many days are giv'n, they do not die till
 late.

Unto all sons of men there is both time and mercy
 given;

Very thankful should we be and strive to enter
 heaven.

When we reach that happy place where the weary
 are at rest;

Xceeding bright and fair we shall be there forever
 blest.

You'll never know a sorrow and will never feel a
 pain;

Zaccheus found the certain way that holy land to
 gain.

Louis' Birthday.

FEBRUARY 22, 1875.

Six years ago this blessed day
  A little angel came
And nestled in my loving breast
  To claim a home and name.

With joyous heart and anxious care
  I've trained his tender mind,
And year to year each natal day
  New buds of promise find.

His prattling tongue and sweet embrace
  Repay my living care,
Life's path would be a dreary road
  Were not my Louis here.

When darkness clouds my troublous sky
  His smiles dispel the gloom,
When sorrow chills my paling cheek
  His voice brings back the bloom.

And as the years still roll along
  Each birthday may be given
That voice, those smiles to cheer me on
  To happiness and heaven.

Jerry.

Alas! poor Jerry's dead,
  His days on earth are o'er,
His wagging tail and laughing eyes
  We ne'er shall see them more.

And tho' no sculptured stone
  Above his head shall rise,
Although no weeping friends strew flowers
  Above where Jerry lies;

Yet, one lone heart, at least,
  His death will long regret;
His meekness and affection sweet,
  She cannot soon forget.

And tho' his humble deeds
  In hist'ry will not live,
At least one humble, grateful lyre
  A tribute tune will give.

So rest in peace, loved Jerry,
  No cares disturb thy rest;
For, while alive, we all allow,
  Of dogs thou wert the best.

To Louis.

In memory of this happy day,
I write a little roundelay;
A holiday in ev'ry State;
Birthday of Washington, the great.

'Tis not of him I wish to write,
But one to memory just as bright;
My darling son, my lovely boy,
My pride, my hope, my life, my joy.

Ten years have winged their happy flight,
Since first my Louis saw the light.
Ten years, with all a mother's pride,
To store his mind aright I've tried.

And now to make this day more dear,
The cherished day of all the year,
I give to him with great delight
The finest present in his sight.

And as each birthday comes around,
Oh, may my Louis still be found,
Growing in goodness as in size,
More worthy of a better prize.

FEBRUARY 22, 1879.

Home.

How dear to each heart is the memory of home,
    How sacred the ties that still bind us;
Though far from its threshold in life we may roam
Its scenes will be with us across the deep foam
    And in joy or sorrow will find us.

There is not in this world a spot that's so sweet
    Or so free from all sorrow and care
As to make us forget that hallowed retreat
Where brothers and sisters in kindness did meet
    And our father and mother were there.

Sweet memories will come and a tear will oft start,
    And a sigh unbidden will rise,   [part
And we long for those pleasures that youth did im-
And those fond recollections well up in the heart
    As we long for our home and its ties.

Education.

"A babe in a house is a well-spring of pleasure"
    Sent down from the regions above,
We hail it with joy as the heart's richest treasure,
    And give it the heart's purest love.

Here innocence dwells with us mortals below,
    A link between angels and men,
The holiest blessing that God can bestow,
    But e'er long He will claim it again.

It is lent to us here as a talent of trust;
    Remember 't is lent and not given;
For we must return it with interest just,
    For of such is the kingdom of heaven.

Though a babe in a house is a sacred delight
    It is also an object of care,
And demands our attention by day and by night;
    The bitter and sweet we must share.

In infancy's hours we must sow the first seed,
    In the cradle its lessons begin,
Obedience and patience at the breast it doth feed,
    To protect it from folly and sin.

The prayers of its mother it will not forget,
　But sweet recollections impart,
And the memory will bring it no after regret,
　But be like sweet balm to his heart.

First seeds of instruction in deep furrows fall,
　When his mind is plastic and soft;
Then instill in his mind as the noblest of all,
　Ambition to soar up aloft.

If you wish to inscribe on life's future page
　Some good that your own hands have done,
Then impress on his mind while in earliest age,
　'Twill appear in the life of your son.

Thus for weal or for woe every word, act or look
　Is written in characters bold,
To be read in the future—the author's own book,
　Then write it in letters of gold.

'Tis true education forms everyone's mind,
　Then early to wisdom attend,
As the young twig is bent so the tree is inclined,
　The good shall endure to the end.

Memory.

[The following lines were suggested by an invitation to attend a reunion of pupils.]

As fond memory reverts to the scenes of my youth,
  Though in far distant lands I now roam,
I see as a vision in the mirage of truth,
  My happy, my dearly loved home.

And Oh, I regret the great distance that parts
  Me from the reunion of friends,
But 'tis sweet to commune with the past in our hearts
  And the thought that with memory blends.

My teachers and schoolmates I think of with pleasure,
  My tasks that were blended with play,
All dwell in my heart as a long-cherished treasure,
  To cheer me till life's closing day.

How oft I have sighed to be young once again,
  To enjoy the sweet memories of old;
But alas, they are passed, and the wish is in vain,
  Youth cannot be purchased with gold.

And here as I sit in my cot by the sea,
  And hear the waves beat on the shore,
I think of the past and what still is to be,
  Until time shall know me no more.

Time Destroys Everything.

Time waits for none, but onward in its flight
Turns youth to age and morning into night;
Along its track destruction may be seen,
Where scarce a vestige tells of what has been.
The mighty monarch, whether base or just,
Soon lowly lieth crumbling in the dust;
The lofty steeple towering to the skies,
Yields to decay and soon in ruin lies;
The noble ship that plows the pathless deep,
Soon will be wrecked into a shapeless heap.
Thus all the works of man's ambitious pride
Are swept away by a resistless tide.
The statesman labors for a nation's praise,
But Time destroys him in his useful days;
The poet strives to win a deathless fame,
Passes away and men forget his name.
The glorious things of earth thus pass away,
Devouring Time claims all things for his prey.
But one sweet thing, as Time itself will prove,
Can never have an end, and that is love.

Fortune Favors the Brave.

I give you a motto to lead you through life,
  Which many a sorrow will save,
No matter how gloomy or bitter the strife:—
  "Fortune will favor the brave."

Oh, mariner tossed on the dark stormy sea,
  Your vessel engulfed by each wave;
Don't give up the ship, tho' all others may flee,
  "Fortune will favor the brave."

Poor trav'ler, o'ertaken by night and by storm,
  With no shelter, perhaps, but a cave ;
Remember this motto, and wait for the morn,
  "Fortune will favor the brave."

Tired merchant, bow'd over your papers and books,
  When all efforts seemed pow'rless to save,
Be steadfast, no matter how gloomy it looks;
  "Fortune will favor the brave."

Fond mother, heart-broken with sorrow and grief,
  Thy jewel just laid in the grave ;
Weep not, God will give you a present relief,
  "Fortune will favor the brave."

Poor, desolate creature, whoever you are,
  Though forsaken—misfortune's poor slave!
Hope, kindled by faith, be thy sure guiding star,
  "Fortune will favor the brave."

Harold's Birthday.

'Tis just one year ago to-day; oh, blessed morn,
My darling little Harold, you were born;
And as I watch you playing by my side
My heart clings to thee, with a mother's pride.

One year to-day, with happy memories fraught
Of happy hours my baby's presence brought,
A constant comfort to my heart has given;
My baby was a sacred gift from heaven.

His faultless form and face divine, to me
Are all a mother's fondest hopes can be;
And the bright lustre of his eyes impart
The latent brilliance of his infant heart.

And as from year to year this day rolls round,
May each one brighter than the last be found;
And each succeeding birthday hail with joy,
While heavenly blessings crown my darling boy.

August 31, 1873.

Love.

"A volume in a word, an ocean in a tear,"
A story without end that angels love to hear,
A heaven in a glance, a whirlwind in a sigh:—
The word, the king of words, the word that cannot die.

What concentrated joy there is in blessed love—
The heart's own sacred music caught from above;
It is a sweet idolatry enslaving all the soul,
The devotion of the heart beyond the heart's control.

It is a fragrant blossom that ever doth impart
Sweet odors that do gladden the garden of the heart;
It is the brightness of affection, and ever is in bloom,
And fadeth not, though planted by the silent tomb.

I have seen its budding beauty, I've felt its magic
    smile,
I have knelt down and kissed it, and laughed and
    wept the while ;
I thought some cherub angel had planted there a
    flower
To flourish for awhile, away from Eden's bower.

This fragrant flower, when blighted, will bud no
    more,
Or shed its odors sweet on Time's unfruitful shore;
This song, when once forgotten, cannot be learned
    again,
The heart can ne'er recall the sacred heavenly strain.

ope.

Hope is the anchor that our bark must save,
While tossed upon this life's tempestuous wave;
And when the billows loudest round us roar,
Hope bids us cling the tighter to our oar.

Though fortune, health, and friendship all do fail,
Yet hope still bids us spread our trembling sail;
And when our bark the storm has wrecked at last,
Hope finds us closely clinging to the mast.

Frail mariner upon the sea of life—
Thy path beset with sorrow, care, and strife;
When troubles come, hope soothes thy sad repining,
For darkest clouds have all a silver lining.

When death knocks at thy door, no power can save;
Hope tells thee life is all beyond the grave;
Hope, as a sovereign balm, to us is given,
To heal our wounds and point the way to heaven.

The Boys.

Here come the boys! Oh, dear, the noise,
   The whole house feels the racket;
Behold the knees of Louie's pants,
   And weep o'er Harold's jacket!

But never mind, if eyes keep bright,
   And limbs grow straight and limber;
I'd rather lose the tree's whole bark
   Than find unsound the timber.

Now hear the tops and marbles roll!
   The floors—oh, woe betide them!
And I must watch the bannisters—
   I know the boys who ride them!

Look well as you descend the stairs—
   I often find them haunted,
By ghostly toys, that make no noise,
   Just when the noise is wanted.

The very chairs are tied in pairs,
   And made to prance and caper;
What swords are whittled out of sticks,
   What brave hats made of paper!

The dinner bell peals loud and well,
  To tell the milkman's coming,
And then the rush of steam-car trains
  Sets all our ears a-humming.

How oft I say, "What shall I do
  To keep these children quiet?"
If I could find a recipe,
  I certainly would try it.

But what to do with these wild boys,
  And all their din and clatter,
Is really quite a grave affair—
  No laughing, trifling matter.

" Boys will be boys," but not for long—
  Ah, could we bear about us
This thought: how very soon our boys
  Will learn to do without us!

How soon the tall and deep-voiced men
  Will gravely call us " Mother!"
Or we be stretching empty hands
  From this world to another.

More gently should we chide the noise,
  And when night quells the racket,
Stitch in, with loving thoughts and prayers,
  While mending pants and jacket.

One Touch of Nature.

A lark's song dropped from heaven,
    A rose's breath at noon,
A still, sweet stream that flows
    Beneath a still, sweet moon.

A little way-side flower
    Plucked from the grasses thus,
A sound, a breath, a glance, and yet
    What is't they bring to us?

For the world grows far too wise,
    And wisdom is but grief;
Much thought makes but a weary way,
    And question, unbelief.

Thank God for the bird's song
    And for the flower's breath,
Thank God for any voice to wake
    The old sweet hymn of faith.

For a world grown all too wise—
    Or is't not wise enough?
Thank God for anything that makes
    The path less dark and rough.

Tired Mothers.

A little elbow leans upon your knee—
    Your tired knee that has so much to bear;
A child's dear eyes are looking lovingly
    From underneath a thatch of tangled hair.
Perhaps you do not heed the velvet touch
    Of warm, moist fingers, holding you so tight;
You do not prize this blessing overmuch ;
    You almost are too tired to pray to-night.

But it *is* blessedness!   A year ago
    I did not see it as I do to-day—
We are so dull and thankless ; and too slow
    To catch the sunshine till it slips away.
And now it seems surpassing strange to me,
    That, while I wore the badge of motherhood,
I did not kiss more oft and tenderly
    The little child that brought me only good.

And if, some night, when you sit down to rest,
    You miss this elbow from your tired knee—
This restless, curling head from off your breast—
    This lisping tongue that chatters constantly ;
If from your own the dimpled hands had slipped,
    And ne'er would nestle in your palm again ;
If the white feet into their grave had tripped,
    I could not blame you for your heart-ache then!

I wonder so that mothers ever fret
   At little children clinging to their gown ;
Or that the foot-prints when the days are wet,
   Are ever black enough to make them frown.
If I could find a little muddy boot,
   Or cap, or jacket, on my chamber floor;
If I could kiss a rosy, restless foot,
   And hear it patter in my home once more ;

If I could mend a broken cart to-day—
   To-morrow make a kite to reach the sky,
There is no woman in God's world could say
   She was more blissfully content than I.
But, ah! the dainty pillow next my own
   Is never rumpled by a shining head ;
My singing birdling from its nest is flown ;
   The little boy I used to kiss is dead!

The Baby.

Where did you come from, Baby, dear?
Out of everywhere into here.

Where did you get your eyes so blue?
Out of the sky as I came through.

Where did you get that little tear?
I found it waiting when I got here.

What makes your forehead so smooth and high?
A soft hand stroked it as I went by.

What makes your cheek like a warm white rose?
I saw something better than anyone knows.

Whence that three-cornered smile of bliss?
Three angels gave me at once a kiss.

Where did you get that pretty ear?
God spoke and it came out to hear.

Where did you get those arms and hands?
Love made itself into hooks and bands.

Feet, whence did you come, you darling things?
From the same box as the cherub's wings.

How did they all come just to you?
God thought of me and so I grew.

But how did you come to us, you dear?
God thought about you and so I am here.

Mother's Boys.

I know there are stains on my carpet,
 The traces of small, muddy boots;
I see your fair tapestry glowing,
 All spotted with blossoms and fruits.

I know that my walls are disfigured
 With prints of small fingers and hands,
And that your own household so neat, in
 Immaculate purity stands.

I know that my parlor is littered
 With many old treasures and toys,
While yours is in daintiest order,
 Unharmed by the presence of boys.

I know that my room is invaded
 Quite boldly all hours of the day,
While you sit in yours, unmolested,
 And dream the soft quiet away.

I know there are three little bedsides,
 Where I must stand watchful each night,
While you can go out in your carriage,
 And flash in your dresses, so bright.

39

I think I'm a neat little woman—
　　I like my home orderly, too;
I'm fond of all dainty belongings,
　　Yet would not change places with you.

No! keep your fair home, with its order,
　　Its freedom from bother and noise,
And keep your own fanciful leisure,
　　But give me my three splendid boys!

To the Memory of My Father.

I had a father once, tender and kind,
Who in his feelings and affections too,
Was gentle as a woman—pure and true.
A mellow radiance beamed ever forth
From his soft eye—pure as our native skies,
Speaking the language of a generous heart
That throbbed within his breast; no stranger passed
Unnoticed by his hospitable board.
His hand was ever ready to bestow
Blessings and alms upon the suffering poor ;
And thus, by generous deeds and noble acts,
He won the love and praise of every heart.
My pen would prove too weak and frail a thing
To picture all the virtues of his soul—
The purity and honor that were his.

But Death, the tyrant monarch, claimed the prize ;
He set the icy signet upon his brow,—
And thus he marked him for his own.
The love-light faded from his eye of blue,
The beauteous smile that ever played around
The rosy lip, vanished at Death's touch.

The heart that beat within that manly breast,
Whose every throb but counted some good deed;
Whose impulses were great and noble—all
Were stilled, and stilled forever.
Remorseless Death! Thy hand hath crushed the hopes
Of many hearts, like fair and fragile flowers
Beneath the feet of the great destroyer—Time.

My father! Oh, what sunny memories cling
Around thy spotless name!
Yes, golden memories of my father dear
Will ever linger in this wayward heart—
Breaking like sunbeams through the clouds of life.
The recollections of thy name are shrined
In sacredness, and kept from the world's gaze,
And ever linked with my sublimest thoughts,
Wakening sweet music in my untaught heart,
Which steals upon the air in cadence soft,
Breathing sweet melody, like some lost strain
In wantonness had wandered off from heaven.

Rock Me to Sleep, Mother.

Backward, turn backward, O Time, in your flight,
Make me a child again, just for to-night!
Mother, come back from the echoless shore,
Take me again to your heart as of yore;
Kiss from my forehead the furrows of care,
Smooth the few silver threads out of my hair;
Over my slumbers your loving watch keep;—
Rock me to sleep, mother,—rock me to sleep!

Backward, flow backward, O tide of the years!
I am so weary of toil and of tears;
Toil without recompense, tears all in vain;
Take them, and give me my childhood again!
I have grown weary of dust and decay,—
Weary of flinging my soul-wealth away;
Weary of sowing for others to reap;—
Rock me to sleep, mother,—rock me to sleep!

Tired of the hollow, the base, the untrue,
Mother, O mother, my heart calls for you!
Many a summer the grass has grown green,
Blossomed and faded, our faces between:

43

Yet with strong yearning and passionate pain,
Long I to-night for your presence again.
Come from the silence so long and so deep;—
Rock me to sleep, mother,—rock me to sleep!

Over my heart in the days that are flown,
No love like mother-love ever has shown;
No other worship abides and endures,
Faithful, unselfish and patient like yours:
None like a mother can charm away pain
From the sick soul, and the world-weary brain.
Slumber's soft calms o'er my heavy lids creep;—
Rock me to sleep, mother,—rock me to sleep!

Come, let your brown hair, just lighted with gold,
Fall on your shoulders again, as of old;
Let it drop over my forehead to-night,
Shading my faint eyes away from the light;
For with its sunny-edged shadows once more,
Haply will throng the sweet visions of yore;
Lovingly, softly, its bright billows sweep;—
Rock me to sleep, mother,—rock me to sleep!

Mother, dear mother, the years have been long
Since I last listened your lullaby song;
Sing, then, and unto my soul it shall seem
Womanhood's years have been only a dream;
Clasped to your heart in a loving embrace,
With your light lashes just sweeping my face,
Never hereafter to wake or to weep;—
Rock me to sleep, mother,—rock me to sleep!

Answer.

My child, my child! thou art weary to-night;
Thy spirit is sad and dim is the light;
Thou wouldst call me back from the silent shore,
To the trials of life, to thy heart as of yore;
Thou longest again for the loving care
For my kiss on thy lips, my hand on thy hair;
But angels around thee, their loving watch keep,
And angels, my child, will rock thee to sleep.

Backward? say, Onward, ye swift rolling years;
Gird on thy armor! Dry up thy tears!
Count not thy trials, nor efforts, in vain,
They'll bring thee the light of thy childhood again.
Ye should not weary, my child, by the way,
But watch for the light of that brighter day;
Not tired of "Sowing for others to reap,"
For angels, my child, will rock thee to sleep.

Nearer thee, now, than in days that are flown
Purer the love-light encircling thy home;
Far more enduring the watch o'er thy sleep,
Than even earth worship, no matter how deep.
Soon the dark shadows will linger no more,
Nor come at thy call, from the opening door;
But know, weary child, the angels, watch keep,
And soon, very soon, will rock thee to sleep.

45

Our Dead.

Nothing is our own; we hold our pleasures
　　Just a little while ere they are fled;
One by one life robs us of our treasures;
　　Nothing is our own except our dead.

They are ours, and hold in faithful keeping,
　　Safe forever, all they took away;
Cruel life can never stir that sleeping,
　　Cruel time can never seize that prey.

Justice pales, truth fades, stars fall from heaven;
　　Human are the great whom we revere;
No true crown of honor can be given
　　Till the wreath lies on a funeral bier.

How the children leave us! and no traces
　　Linger of that smiling angel band;
Gone, forever gone—and in their places
　　Weary men and anxious women stand.

Yet we have some little ones, still ours;
　　They have kept the baby smile we know,
Which we kissed one day, and hid with flowers,
　　On their dead white faces long ago.

46

When our joy is lost—and life will take it—
　Then no memory of the past remains,
Save with some strange, cruel stings, that make it
　Bitterness beyond all present pains.

Death, more tender-hearted, leaves to sorrow
　Still the radiant shadow—fond regret;
We shall find, in some far, bright to-morrow,
　Joy that he has taken, living yet.

Is love ours, and do we dream we know it?
　Bound with all our heart-strings, all our own ?
Any cold and cruel dawn may show it
　Shattered, desecrated, overthrown.

Only the dead hearts forsake us never;
　Love, that to Death's loyal care has fled,
Is thus consecrated ours forever,
　And no change can rob us of our dead.

So, when fate comes to besiege our city,
　Dim our gold, or make our flowers fall,
Death, the angel, comes in love and pity,
　And, to save our treasures, claims them all.

A Mother's Heart.

A little dreaming, such as mothers know;
    A little lingering over dainty things;
A happy heart, wherein hope all aglow
    Strikes like a bird at dawn that wakes and sings—
        And that is all.

A little clasping to her yearning breast,
    A little musing over future years;
A heart that prays, "Dear Lord, thou knowest best,
    But spare my flower life's bitterest rain of tears"—
        And that is all.

A little spirit speeding through the night;
    A little home grown lonely, dark and chill;
A sad heart groping blindly for the light;
    A little snow-clad grave beneath the hill—
        And that is all.

A little gathering of life's broken thread;
    A little patience keeping back the tears;
A heart that sings, "Thy darling is not dead,
    God keeps him safe through his eternal years."
        And that is all.

Retrospection.

A peaceful home, a sun-lit land,
　A lad that careless went his way;
A comfort kind on every hand,
　Each wish fulfilled from day to day;
A mother's face, so wondrous fair,
　A mother's love, so warm and true—
But youth knew not its treasures there,
　And sought the world and pleasures new.

A score of years (so quickly flown),
　Of sorrows dark, of pleasures bright;
A lonely mound, a simple stone,
　With "Mother" writ in letters white;
An honored man, a royal fame,
　Ambition's prize on every side;
A princely wealth, a lauded name,
　And all that flatters human pride.

But fame was hollow, wealth was dross;
　Of little worth the pride of place;
And naught could compensate the loss—
　The ne'er-forgotten mother's face.
He learned, as learn it all men must,
　For every life its truth doth prove—
The brightest gem, the dearest trust
　Vouchsafed to man—a mother's love.

The Empty Cradle.

Sad is the heart of the mother,
  Who sits by the lonely hearth,
Where never again the children
  Shall waken their songs of mirth,
And still through the painful silence
  She listens for voice and tread;
Outside of the heart—there only
  She knows that they are not dead!

Here is the desolate cradle,
  The pillow so lately pressed,
But far away has the birdling
  Flown from its little nest.
Crooning the lullabies over
  That once were the babe's delight,
All through the misty spaces
  She follows its upward flight.

Little she thought of a moment
  So gloomy and sad as this,
When close to her heart she gathered
  Her child for its good-night kiss.

He should be tenderly cherished,
    Never a grief should he know;
Wealth, and the pride of a prince,
    These would a mother bestow.

And this is the darling's portion
    In heaven—where he has fled;
By angels securely guarded,
    By angels securely led.
Brooding in sorrowful silence
    Over the empty nest.
Can you not see through the shadows
    Why it is all for the best?

Eyes.

Sweet baby eyes
They look around with such a grave surprise,
What do you see?
A strange new world, where simplest things
Engender wild imaginings
And fancies free?
A resting place that is not home,
A paradise wherein to roam,
For years, may be?
O placid, wondering baby eyes,
The mystery that in you lies
Oft puzzles me.

Clear, boyish eyes,
Whose fearless glance unconsciously defies
Trouble and care;
When babyhood is past and gone,
What is it that you gaze upon?
A land most fair;
A sunny shore with pleasure rife;
And that great glorious gift of life
'Tis bliss to share,

O happy, trustful, boyish eyes,
Let sages envy, fools despise,
  The faith you wear.

   The anxious eyes
Of manhood, slowly piercing earth's disguise,
  Discover—what?
That life at best is quickly done,
That hopes fulfilled and wishes won
  Are dearly got;
That shadows chased in headlong haste,
And golden fruit he strove to taste,
  Delight him not.
O, restless, doubting, troubled eyes,
To learn in sorrow to be wise
  Is manhood's lot.

   Dim, aged eyes,
Gazing across the wreck of broken ties,
  What do they see?
Behind—dead leaves that withered fall,
A fading wilderness where all
  Is vanity;
Before—to gladden weary sight,
A glimpse, a promise of the bright
  Eternity.
O dim and tearful aged eyes,
If waiting till that dawn shall rise,
  Blessed are ye!

And angel eyes,
Who have their dwelling-place beyond the skies,
Vainly do we
Imagine the glories they must know,
Picture the Pearly gates aglow—
The crystal sea
For brightest visions mortal paint
Of that celestial country, faint
Must ever be.
No! pure and holy eyes,
We can but pray that what you prize
Our own may see.

The Unfinished Prayer.

—

[It is said of JOHN QUINCY ADAMS that he never went to bed without repeating this little prayer, the first taught him by the mother whose
memory was so dear to him to the last.]

Golden head so lowly bending,
    Little feet so white and bare,
Dewy eyes, half shut, half open,
    Lisping out his evening prayer.

"Now I lay"—repeat it, darling—
    "Lay me," lisped the tiny lips
Of my darling, kneeling, bending
    O'er the folded finger tips.

"Down to sleep"—"To sleep," he murmured,
    And the curly head bent low;
"I pray the Lord"—I gently added,
    "You can say it all I know."

"Pray the Lord"—the sound came faintly,
    Fainter still—"My soul to keep."
Then the tired head fairly nodded
    And the child was fast asleep.

But the dewy eyes half opened
   When I clasped him to my breast,
And the dear voice softly whispered,
    "Mamma, God knows all the rest."

O, the rapture, sweet unbroken,
   Of the soul who wrote that prayer!
Children's myriad voices floating
   Up to Heaven, record it there.

If of all that has been written,
   I could choose what might be mine,
It should be that child's petition
   Rising to the throne divine.

An Order for a Picture.

O good painter, tell me true,
　　Has your hand the cunning to draw
　　Shapes of things that you never saw?
Ay? Well, here is an order for you.

Woods and cornfields a little brown,—
　　The picture must not be over-bright,
　　Yet all in the golden and gracious light
Of a cloud, when the summer sun is down.
　　Alway and alway, night and morn,
　　Woods upon woods, with fields of corn
　　　Lying between them, not quite sere,
And not in the full, thick, leafy bloom,
When the wind can hardly find breathing-room
　　　Under their tassels,—cattle near,
Biting shorter the short green grass,
And a hedge of sumach and sassafras,
With bluebirds twittering all around,—
(Ah, good painter, you can't paint sound!)
　　These, and the house where I was born,
Low and little, and black and old,
With children, many as it can hold,

All at the windows, open wide,—
Heads and shoulders clear outside,
And fair young faces all ablush:
    Perhaps you may have seen, some day,
    Roses crowding the self-same way,
Out of a wilding, wayside bush.

    Listen closer.   When you have done
      With woods and cornfields and grazing herds,
    A lady, the loveliest ever the sun
Looked down upon, you must paint for me;
Oh, if I only could make you see
The clear blue eyes, the tender smile,
The sovereign sweetness, the gentle grace,
The woman's soul, and the angel's face
    That are beaming on me all the while,
    I need not speak these foolish words:
    Yet one word tells you all I would say,—
She is my mother: you will agree
    That all the rest may be thrown away.

Two little urchins at her knee
You must paint, sir; one like me,
    The other with a clearer brow,
    And the light of his adventurous eyes
    Flashing with boldest enterprise:
At ten years old he went to sea,—
    God knoweth if he be living now;
    He sailed in the good ship "Commodore,"—
Nobody ever crossed her track

To bring us news, and she never came back.
　　Ah, 'tis twenty long years and more
Since that old ship went out of the bay
　　With my great-hearted brother on her deck:
　　I watched him till he shrank to a speck,
And his face was toward me all the way.
Bright his hair was, a golden brown,
　　The time we stood at our mother's knee:
That beauteous head, if it did go down,
　　Carried sunshine into the sea!

Out in the fields one summer night
　　We were together, half afraid
　　Of the corn-leaves' rustling, and of the shade
Of the high hills, stretching so still and far,—
Afraid to go home, sir; for one of us bore
A nest full of speckled and thin-shelled eggs ;
The other, a bird, held fast by the legs,
Not so big as a straw of wheat:
The berries we gave her she wouldn't eat,
But cried and cried, till we held her bill,
So slim and shining, to keep her still.

At last we stood at our mother's knee.
　　Do you think, sir, if you try,
　　You can paint the look of a lie?
　　If you can, pray have the grace
　　To put it solely in the face
Of the urchin that is likest me:
　　I think 'twas solely mine, indeed:

But that's no matter,—paint it so;
    The eyes of our mother—(take good heed)—
Looking not on the nestful of eggs,
Nor the fluttering bird, held so fast by the legs,
But straight through our faces down to our lies,
And oh, with such injured, reproachful surprise!
    I felt my heart bleed where that glance went,
               As though
A sharp blade struck through it.
               You, sir, know
That you on the canvas are to repeat
Things that are fairest, things most sweet,—
Woods and cornfields and mulberry tree,—
The mother, the lads, with their bird, at her knee:
    But, oh, that look of reproachful woe!
High as the heavens your name I'll shout,
If you paint me the picture, and leave that out.

If We Knew.

If we knew the woe and heartache
    Waiting for us down the road,
If our lips could taste the wormwood,
    If our backs could feel the load,
Would we waste to-day in wishing
    For a time that ne'er can be?
Would we wait in such impatience
    For our ships to come from sea?

If we knew the baby fingers
    Pressed against the window pane
Would be cold and stiff to-morrow—
    Never trouble us again.
Would the bright eyes of our darling
    Catch the frown upon our brow?
Would the print of rosy fingers
    Vex us then as it does now?

Ah! those little ice-cold fingers,
    How they point our memory back
To the hasty words and actions
    Strewn along our backward track!

How these little hands remind us,
As in snowy grace they lie,
Not to scatter thorns, but roses,
For our reaping by-and-by!

Strange we never prize the music
Till the sweet-voiced bird has flown;
Strange that we should slight the violets
Till the lovely flowers are gone;
Strange that Summer skies and sunshine
Never seem one half so fair
As when Winter's snowy pinions
Shake their white down in the air!

Lips from which the seal of silence
None but God can roll away,
Never blossomed in such beauty
As adorns the mouth to-day;
And sweet words that freight our memory
With their beautiful perfume,
Come to us in sweetest accents
Through the portals of the tomb.

Let us gather up the sunbeams
Lying all along our path;
Let us keep the wheat and roses,
Casting out the thorns and chaff;
Let us find our sweetest comfort
In the blessings of to-day,
With a patient hand removing
All our griefs from out our way.

In the Nest.

Gather them close to your heart,
    Cradle them on your breast; .
They will soon enough leave your brooding care,
Soon enough mount youth's topmost stair,
    Little ones in the nest.

Fret not that the children's hearts are gay,
    That the restless feet will run;
There may come a time in the bye and bye,
When you'll sit in your lonely room and sigh
    For a sound of childish fun;

When you'll long for the repetition sweet
    That sounded through each room,
Of "Mother, mother," the dear love-calls
That will echo loud in the silent halls,
    And add to their stately gloom.

There may come a time when you'll long to hear
    The eager boyish tread,
The tuneless whistle, the clear, shrill shout,
The busy bustle in and out,
    And pattering overhead.

Then gather them close to your loving heart,
    Cradle them on your breast;
They will soon enough leave your brooding care,
Soon enough mount youth's topmost stair,
    Little ones in the nest.

Little Feet.

Two little feet, so small that both may nestle
    In one caressing hand—
Two tender feet upon the untried border
    Of life's mysterious land.

Dimpled and soft, and pink as peach-tree blossoms,
    In April's fragrant days,
How can they walk among the briery tangles
    Edging the world's rough ways?

These rose-white feet along the doubtful future
    Must bear a manly load;
Alas! Since man has the heaviest burden,
    And walks the harder road!

Love, for awhile, will make the path before them
    All dainty, smooth and fair—
Will cull away the brambles, letting only
    The roses blossom there.

But when the mother's watchful eyes are shrouded
    Away from sight of men,
And these dear feet are left without her guiding,
    Who shall direct them then?

How will they be allured, betrayed, deluded,
    Poor little untaught feet!
Into what dreary mazes will they wander,
    What dangers will they meet?

Will they go stumbling blindly in the darkness
    Of sorrow's tearful shades?
Or find the upland slopes of Peace and Beauty,
    Whose sunlight never fades?

Will they go toiling up Ambition's summit,
    The common world above?
Or in some nameless vale, securely sheltered,
    Walk side by side with Love?

Some feet there be which walk life's track unwounded,
    Which find but pleasant ways:
Some hearts there be to which this life is only
    A round of happy days.

But they are few. Far more there are who wander
    Without a hope or friend—
Who find their journey full of pains and losses,
    And long to reach the end.

How shall it be with him, the tender stranger,
  Fair-faced and gentle-eyed,
Before whose unstained feet the world's rude highway
  Stretches so far and wide?

Ah! who may read the future? For our darling
  We crave all blessings sweet,
And pray that He who feeds the crying ravens
  Will guide the baby's feet.

The Silver Lining.

There's never a day so sunny
But a little cloud appears;
There's never a life so happy
But has had its time of tears;
Yet the sun shines out the brighter
When the stormy tempest clears.

There's never a garden growing
With roses in every plot;
There's never a heart so hardened
But it has one tender spot;
We have only to prune the border
To find the forget-me-not.

There's never a cup so pleasant
But has bitter with the sweet;
There's never a path so rugged
That bears not the prints of feet;
And we have a helper promised
For the trials we may meet.

There's never a sun that rises
But we know 'twill set at night;
The tints that gleam in the morning

At evening are just as bright;
And the hour that is the sweetest
Is between the dark and light.

There's never a dream that's happy
But the waking makes us sad;
There's never a dream of sorrow
But the waking makes us glad;
We shall look some day with wonder
At the troubles we have had.

There's never a way so narrow
But the entrance is made straight;
There's always a guide to point us
To the "little wicker gate;"
And the angels will be nearer
To a soul that is desolate.

There's never a heart so haughty
But will some day bow and kneel;
There's never a heart so wounded
That the Saviour cannot heal;
There's many a lowly forehead
That is bearing the hidden seal.

Seven Times One.

There's no dew left on the daisies and clover,
  There's no rain left in heaven.
I've said my " Seven times " over and over—
  Seven times one are seven.

I am old—so old I can write a letter;
  My birthday lessons are done.
The lambs play always—they know no better;
  They are only one times one.

O Moon! in the night I have seen you sailing
  And shining so round and low.
You were bright, ah, bright!—but your light is failing;
  You are nothing now but a bow.

You Moon, have you done something wrong in heaven,
  That God has hidden your face?
I hope, if you have, you will soon be forgiven,
  And shine again in your place.

O velvet Bee! you 're a dusty fellow—
  You 've powdered your legs with gold.
O brave marsh Mary-buds, rich and yellow,
  Give me your money to hold !

O columbine! open your folded wrapper,
    Where two twin turtle-doves dwell!
O cuckoo-pint! toll me the purple clapper
    That hangs in your clear green bell!

And show me your nest, with the young ones in it —
    I will not steal them away:
I am old! you may trust me, linnet, linnet!
    I am seven times one to-day.

The Essence of Life.

Fair are the flowers and the children, but their subtle
    suggestion is fairer;
Rare is the rose-burst of dawn, but the secret that
    clasps it is rarer;
Sweet the exultance of song, but the strain that pre-
    cedes it is sweeter,
And never was poem yet writ, but the meaning out-
    masters the meter.

Never a daisy that grows, but a mystery guideth the
    growing;
Never a river that flows, but a majesty scepters the
    flowing;
Never a Shakespeare that soared, but a stronger than
    he did enfold him;
Nor ever a prophet foretells, but a mightier seer hath
    foretold him.

Back of the canvas that throbs, the painter is hinted
    and hidden;
Into the statue that breathes, the soul of the sculptor
    is bidden;

71

Under the joy that is felt, lie the infinite issues of
    feeling;
Crowning the glory revealed, is the glory that crowns
    the revealing.

Great are the symbols of being, but that which is
    symboled is greater;
Vast the create and beheld, but vaster the inward
    Creator;
Back of the sound broods the silence, back of the gift
    stands the giving;
Back of the hand that receives, thrill the sensitive
    nerves of receiving.

  And up from the pits where these shiver,
    And up from the hights where those shine,
  Twin voices and shadows swim starward,
    And the essence of life is divine.

The Secret Prayer.

A single grateful thought towards Heaven is the most perfect prayer.

It was a still and silent hour
    In an isle on the southern seas,
And slowly the shades of night were swept
    Away by the morning breeze,
When a lowly son of Britain stood
    With cheek and brow of care,
Seeking amid the solitude,
    A place for secret prayer.

No ear to hear in that silent glen,
    No eye but the eye of God,
But the giant fern gave back a voice
    As forth the wanderer trod.
They were broken words that met his ear,
    But a name was mingled there,
It was the name of Christ he heard,
    And the language of secret prayer.

A native of that savage isle
    From the depths of his full heart cried,
For mercy, for help in the hour of need,
    For faith in the crucified;

And peace and hope were in those tones
   So solemnly sweet they were;
For He who answers while yet we call,
   Had heard that secret prayer.

The morning dawned on that lonely spot,
   But a far more glorious day
Came with the accents of prayer and praise,
   On the Indian's lip that lay,
The first, the first who had called on God
   In those regions of Satan's care;
The first who had breath'd in his native tongue,
   The language of secret prayer.

And he who that hallow'd music heard
   The missionary lone;
Oh! the joy that thrilled thro' his yearning heart
   By a stranger may not be known;
But he knelt and blessed the hand that sent
   In the hour of his deep despair,
Comfort and strength to his fainting soul,
   With the voice of that secret prayer.

Imaginary Evils.

Let to-morrow take care of to-morrow,
  Leave things of the future to fate;
What use to anticipate sorrow?
  Life's troubles come never too late.

If to hope over-much be an error,
  'Tis one that the wise have preferred;
And how often have hearts been in terror
  Of evils that never occurred.

Have faith, and thy faith shall sustain thee,
  Permit not suspicion and care
With invisible bonds to enchain thee,
  But bear what God gives thee to bear.

By his spirit supported and gladdened,
  And ne'er by " forebodings " deferred—
But think how oft heart have been saddened
  By fear of what never occurred.

Let to-morrow take care of to-morrow;
  Short and dark as our life may appear,
We make it still darker by sorrow—
  Still shorter by folly and fear.

Half our troubles are of our invention,
  And often from blessings conferred
Have we shrunk in vague apprehension
  Of evils that never occurred.

Only Waiting.

Only waiting till the shadows
   Are a little longer grown,
Only waiting till the glimmer
   Of the day's last beam is flown;
Till the night of earth is faded
   From this heart once full of day,
Till the dawn of heaven is breaking
   Through the twilight soft and gray.

Only waiting till the reapers
   Have the last sheaf gathered home,
For the summer-time hath faded
   And the autumn winds are come.
Quickly, reapers, gather quickly
   The last ripe hours of my heart—
For the bloom of life is withered,
   And I hasten to depart.

Only waiting till the angels
   Open wide the mystic gate,
At whose feet I long have lingered,
   Weary, poor, and desolate.

Even now I hear their footsteps
   And their voices far away :
If they call me I am waiting,—
   Only waiting to obey.

Only waiting till the shadows
   Are a little longer grown,
Only waiting till the glimmer
   Of the day's last beam is flown;
Then from out the folded darkness
   Holy, deathless star shall rise,
By whose light my soul will gladly
   Wing her passage to the skies.

Mother, Dec. 31, 1884.

Eugene.

Tread softly! Let no sound disturb the ear;
Let silence reign forever here.
A hallowed sweetness rests upon this spot;
While memory lasts, shall never be forgot;
And every object lingering nigh,
Brings back his image to my eye.
Oh, may these memories ever last
As sacred mementoes of the past.
I sit and view each vacant chair,
And fancy paints him sitting there;
Nor does the fancy slumber here,
His laugh throughout the house I hear,
And echoes from his youthful voice
Make all within my heart rejoice.
Be still!   Oh, do not break the spell,
Nor call him back to earth to dwell.
No brighter star from God was given,
No brighter gem now shines in heaven.

Died, Monterey, Sept. 28, 1873.

Monterey.

I ask no brighter Paradise,
  I seek no fairer land;
There is no purer loveliness
  On any ocean strand
Than this, whose shells the rarest
  I cull each holiday—
Surrounded by the fairest
  Of lovely Monterey.

I've roamed the shores of Italy
  In happy infant years;
Whene'er I think of Ireland,
  Fast fall affection's tears.
But still, I say with candor,
  Dissent from me who may,
Thy shores are fairer, grander,—
  Embowered Monterey.

Fair are the fields of Genoa—
  My boyhood's early home,
Its castellated terraces,
  Each grand majestic dome

Before my mind rise clearly,
  Where'er I chance to stray,
But thou art loved more dearly,
  Majestic Monterey.

The roaring of the Zuider Zee,
  The Leyden loves it well;
The Roman views the Tiber banks
  With thoughts no pen may tell,
But thou art more enchanting
  When the last solar ray
Is o'er thy waters slanting—
  Romantic Monterey.

When taken by necessity,
  For freely I'll ne'er leave,
My troubled heart in bitterness
  With saddened sigh must grieve;
For thy fair crescent waters
  Where I so love to stray
With some—thy fairest daughters,—
  Pacific Monterey.

The waters of Niagara,
  With great majestic roll,
Has filled my mind eternally
  Without my heart's control,
But thy pure peaceful waters
  Must be to me alway,
As pleasing as thy daughters—
  Angelic Monterey.

But Bahia Vista Cottage
  Is far more dear to me,
Than Ireland, than Italy,
  Than roaring Zuider Zee,
Than all the sweets of Genoa,
  Than Tiber's yellow spray,
Than all thy other beauties—
  Enchanting Monterey.

Power of Success.

Laugh, and the world laughs with you;
    Weep, and you weep alone;
For this brave old earth must borrow its mirth,
    It has trouble enough of its own.

Sing, and the hills will answer;
    Sigh, it is lost on the air;
The echoes bound to a joyful sound,
    But shrink from voicing care.

Rejoice, and men will seek you,
    Grieve, and they turn and go;
They want full measure for all your pleasure.
    But do not want your woe.

Be glad, and your friends are many;
    Be sad, and you lose them all.
There are none to decline your nectared wine,
    But alone you must drink life's gall.

Feast, and your halls are crowded;
    Fast, and the world goes by.
Succeed and give, and it helps you to live,
    But no man can help you to die.

There's room in the halls of pleasure
    For a long and lordly train,
But one by one we must all file on
    Thro' the narrow aisles of pain.

Downhearted.

Downhearted? Pshaw! there's seldom seen
  A lane without a turning!
Each desert has a spot of green,
  In spite of bright Sol's burning.
Your friends have left you? Well, what then?
  Remember changing Peter;
Sorrow has tried the best of men,
  And life is all the sweeter.

What adds a zest to summer's joy?
  Is it not a winter weary?
Peace would be tame without alloy,
  Past grief makes solace cheery.
All cannot win though all must run
  When once life's race is started:
Yet all may hear the words: "Well done,"
  So never be downhearted.

A Mother's Gift.

[Written by a mother on the fly-leaf of a Bible—her gift to a son.]

Remember, love, who gave thee this,
   When other days shall come—
When she who had thy earliest kiss,
   Sleeps in the narrow home;
Remember, 'twas a mother gave
The gift to one she'd die to save.

That mother sought a pledge of love,
   The holiest for her son;
And from the gift of God above,
   She chose a godly one;
She chose for her beloved boy
The source of life, and light and joy.

She bade him keep the gift—that when
   The parting hour should come,
They might have hope to meet again,
   In her eternal home.
She said his faith in that would be
Sweet incense to her memory.

And should the scoffer, in his pride,
   Laugh that fond gift to scorn,
And bid him cast his pledge aside
   That he from youth had borne!
She bade him pause and ask his breast,
If he, or she, had loved him best.

A parent's blessing on my son
   Goes with this holy thing;
The love that would retain the one
   Must to the other cling,
Remember, 'tis no idle toy,
A mother's gift—REMEMBER, BOY!

The Golden Side.

There is many a rest in the road through life,
　If we would only stop to take it,
And many a tone from the better land,
　If the querulous heart would make it.
To the soul that is full of hope,
　And whose beautiful trust ne'er faileth,
The grass is green and the flowers are bright,
　Though the Winter's storm prevaileth.

Better to hope, though the clouds hang low,
　And to keep the eyes still lifted;
For the bright blue sky will soon peep through,
　When the ominous clouds are rifted.
There was never a night without a day,
　Or an evening without a morning;
And the darkest hour, so the proverb goes,
　Is the hour before the dawning.

There is many a gem in the path of life
　Which we pass in our idle pleasure,
That is richer far than the jeweled crown,
　Or the miser's hoarded treasure;

It may be the love of a little child,
　Or a mother's prayer to heaven,
Or only a beggar's grateful thanks
　For a cup of water given.

Better to weave in the path of life
　A bright and golden setting,
And to do God's will with a cheerful heart,
　And hands that are ready and willing,
Than to snap the delicate minute thread
　Of our curious lives asunder,
And then blame heaven for the tangled ends,
　And sit, and grieve, and wonder.

Mercy.

"The quality of mercy is not strain'd;
It droppeth as the gentle rain from heaven,
Upon the place beneath: it is twice bless'd;
It blesseth him that gives, and him that takes:
'Tis mightiest in the mightiest; it becomes
The throned monarch better than his crown:
His sceptre shows the force of temporal power,
The attribute to awe and majesty,
Wherein doth sit the dread and fear of kings;
But mercy is above his sceptred sway.
It is enthroned in the hearts of kings,
It is an attribute to God himself;
And earthly power doth then show likest God's
When mercy seasons justice."

Shakespeare's Advice.

[The following selections from different plays giving advice to young men, are copied with a hope that mothers will deeply impress these noble sentiments on the minds of their young sons. They embrace counsel and direction for every state of life from the cradle to the grave:]

Hamlet.

"Give thy thoughts no tongue,
Nor any unproportion'd thought his act.
Be thou familiar, but by no means vulgar.
The friends thou hast, and their adoption tried,
Grapple them to thy soul with hooks of steel;
But do not dull thy palm with entertainment
Of each new-hatch'd unfledg'd comrade. Beware
Of entrance to a quarrel: but, being in,
Bear it, that the opposer may beware of thee.
Give every man thine ear, but few thy voice:
Take each man's censure, but reserve thy judgment.
Costly thy habit as thy purse can buy,
But not expressed in fancy; rich, not gaudy,
For the apparel oft proclaims the man;
And they in France, of the best rank and station,
Are most select and generous, chief in that.

Neither a borrower, nor a lender be,
For loan oft loses both itself and friend;
And borrowing dulls the edge of husbandry.
This above all,—To thine ownself be true.
And it must follow, as the night the day,
Thou canst not then be false to any man."

All's Well That Ends Well.

"Love all, trust a few,
Do wrong to none: be able for thine enemy
Rather in power than use; and keep thy friend
Under thy own life's key: Be checked for silence,
But never taxed for speech."

Julius Cæsar.

"There is a tide in the affairs of men,
Which, taken at the flood, leads on to fortune;
Omitted, all the voyage of their life
Is bound in shallows and in miseries.
On such a full sea are we now afloat,
And we must take the current when it serves,
Or lose our ventures."

Anthony and Cleopatra.

"We, ignorant of ourselves,
Beg often our own harms, which the wise powers
Deny us for our good; so find we profit,
By losing of our prayers."

Hamlet.

"And that should teach us,
There's a divinity that shapes our ends,
Rough-hew them how we will."

" In the corrupted currents of this world
Offence's gilded hand may shove by justice;
And oft 'tis seen, the wicked prize itself
Buys out the law: But 'tis not so above:
There is no shuffling, there the action lies
In his true nature; and we ourselves compell'd,
Even to the teeth and forehead of our faults,
To give in evidence."

Henry VIII.

"I charge thee, fling away ambition;
By that sin fell the angels; how can man then,
The image of his Maker, hope to win by't?
Love thyself last; cherish those hearts that hate thee.
Corruption wins not more than honesty.
Still in thy right hand carry gentle peace,
To silence envious tongues. Be just, and fear not.
Let all the ends thou aim'st at be thy country's,
Thy God's, and truth's; then, if thou fall'st,
Thou fall'st a blessed martyr!"

Hamlet.

"Be thou chaste as ice, as pure as snow, thou shalt not escape calumny."

Julius Cæsar.

"My heart laments that virtue
Cannot live out of the teeth of emulation."

Henry VIII.

" Men that make
Envy, and crooked malice, nourishment,
Dare bite the best.
If I am traduc'd by tongues, which neither know
My faculties nor person, yet will be
The chronicles of my doing,—let me say,
'Tis but the fate of place, and the rough brake
That virtue must go through.   We must not stint
Our necessary actions, in the fear
To cope malicious censurers; which ever
As ravenous fishes, do a vessel follow
That is new trimm'd; but benefit no further
Than vainly longing.   What we oft do best,
By sick interpreters, once weak ones, is
Not ours, or not allow'd; what worst, as oft,
Hitting a grosser quality, is cried up
For our best act.   If we shall stand still,
In fear our motion will be mock'd or carp'd at,
We should take root here where we sit, or sit
State statues only."

Hamlet.

" Meet it is, I set it down,
That one may smile, and smile and be a villain."

Richard III.

"Ah ! that deceit should steal such gentle shapes,
And with a virtuous visor hide deep vice!"

Henry VI.

"What stronger breast-plate than a heart untainted?
Thrice is he armed that hath his quarrel just;
And he but naked, though locked up in steel,
Whose conscience with injustice is corrupted."

Julius Cæsar.

"Cowards die many times before their deaths;
The valiant never taste of death but once.
Of all the wonders that I yet have heard,
It seems to me most strange that men should fear;
Seeing that death, a necessary end,
Will come, when it will come."

Much Ado About Nothing.

"Friendship is constant in all other things,
Save in the office and affairs of love:
Therefore, all hearts in love use their own tongues.
Let every eye negotiate for itself,
And trust no agent: for beauty is a witch
Against whose charms faith melteth into blood."

King Henry VI.

"Let never day nor night unhallow'd pass,
But still remember what the Lord hath done."

Hamlet.

"Confess yourself to heaven;
Repent what's past; avoid what is to come."

Henry IV.

"Oh, gentlemen, the time of life is short;
To spend that shortness basely, were too long,
If life did ride upon a dial's point,
Still ending at the arrival of an hour."

www.ingramcontent.com/pod-product-compliance
Lightning Source LLC
Chambersburg PA
CBHW020033030726
47499CB00007B/2399